MEMORY RECALL (ENGLISH EDITION)

VIJAYKUMAR S KOLI

ISBN 979-888606514-5

"Some memories are such that we can never forget."
And
“Remembrance is such a part of our life, with the help of which we spend our whole life.”

Contents

Preface

Actually I don't know what to say. Still, I have to start somewhere, so I was very fond of watching movies and playing video games, although still there is. Simply put, the same thing as before is no longer in films. And if I say video games, I still play it occasionally.

Although I do not know whether it will be correct to tell or not, but still I do not know why I think it is necessary to tell this thing, so I got this story from a video game, I got the idea. Although the story of that video game is different, and the story of this one is different. And I have written this whole story. This is neither a remake nor a copy. This is just my imagination. And this whole story is fictional. I just got the idea from a game. But I could not understand how to write it. Why did she do that, I had never read any book or any novel. Then I read a book for that, then I got the book 'Harry Potter'. Which I got from internet. Then after reading a few pages of the book of Harry Potter, I got the knowledge of writing, or rather, I understood how to write a book i.e. novel. Still I had a lot to learn. Because, my writing was still not that good, or rather, it is still not that good. You will definitely understand this while reading this book of mine. So I apologize for that. And this is my first book, but still I have tried my best to explain the story. I just want to increase my vocabulary and increase my book from 60/70 pages to 160/260 pages. So for this I have to read and write a lot of books. And this my effort is still going on, and will continue. And I'll keep coming up with more stories. And will keep the readers entertained.

Well, not getting bored anymore. This is where I end my words. And thanks again!! that you bought my book.

And I hope you will like this book.

Yours,
Vijaykumar S Koli

CHAPTER ONE

MEMORY RECALL

It was night time and a boy named 'Abhay Sharma' was a boy around the age of 27. He once worked in a Baar Tender. And was living a good life. But at that time he was going back home after having fun at 12:00 in the night. He was walking drunk on the 'Delhi' highway road. He was wearing a silver hooded T-shirt and black jeans and pants. But suddenly he fainted.

He had a bad dream and he woke up but he was somewhere else. He was in a big hall, and was lying on a big machine. Then a woman and a man were trying to handle him, when 'Abhay' tried to run away from there, but he could not run away because the whole room was closed. That's why he couldn't run.

"Why have I been brought here? And why have you kidnapped me? And who are you guys?" 'Abhay' nervously asked both of them.

"You calm down! We'll tell you all." The man said calmly to 'Abhay'.

"Calm down! Calm down? And why calm down?" 'Abhay' shouted angrily. - "Why have I been brought here after all? Why?"

"We will answer all your questions, first you calm down."

Just like that 'Abhay' calmed down. And then started looking here and there.

He saw that the hall was very big. And the height of the hall was also quite large. And the hall in which he was standing. She was on the top floor. In that hall there was a full goggle glass wall on one side, which showed the full view from inside to outside, but not from outside to inside. And some wall had book set showcase. The machine on which he was lying was glowing with a blue light. That machine was the same length as a single bed. There were many wires on the side of that machine. And there were also some computer screens.

"My name is Professor. 'Shyamlal Mehta' I am a scientist. And this is Nandani Mukherjee, this is the research assistant. And it works for me here. And this machine is also made by me. This is called 'memory recall'. Pro. 'Shyamlal' said keeping his hand on the machine.

That man was about 60 years old. The man was wearing a big coat of white color, like the one that the scientist wears while doing experiments in the laboratory. The man was a little shy in appearance. He was half bald. His beard was completely white.

"What! ... Memory Recall! Meaning?" 'Abhay' asked in surprise.

"Meaning machine to see memories. Yes! This is a machine for seeing memories. With this we can never forget our memories. 'Nandani' said showing hand towards the machine.

Nandani was very beautiful in appearance. Her age was equal to 34, but she looked 26/27 in appearance. He was wearing a black coat and black pants.

"how is it possible? That can never happen." 'Abhay' said with disbelief.

"Why can't it be? Nothing like this can happen in the world of science, everything can happen. 'Pro. Shyamlal said.

"But how so?" 'Abhay' asked in surprise.

"Ok! Let me ask you a simple question. To which you have to give a simple answer. Pro. 'Shyamlal' said.

"Ok! Ask."

"What did you do yesterday?"

Then 'Abhay' starts remembering what he did yesterday.

Seeing him remembering Pro. 'Shyamlal' says to him, "To remember this means to find memories. Meaning that in your mind, when I asked you the question, then you started remembering that you were looking for memories. It means you were looking for memories in your mind, that means you were trying to remember memories. When you remember memories, then you tell what happened yesterday. Meaning that whatever you remember, you tell. Similarly, this machine works in a similar way. And this is the technique I have adopted on this machine. The only difference is that we can never forget anything through this machine."

"How is that?" 'Abhay' asked.

"Because this machine has the technology to bring back the memory. If you say like this, then this is such a machine, through which we can see our memory. Well leave all this... tell me why do we dream? Have you ever wondered why we dream?"

'Abhay' sank in thought for a while and then nodded his head. "I don't know."

"Actually no one has the answer. If so, it's just a theory. Which is generally said that we see dreams because of whatever we see or feel during the day. The same thoughts or same things are shown or seen in our dreams. Basically our brain stores whatever we see during the day in our brain like a memory card... Our conscious brain actually scans those memories while sleeping. And it seems that in reality everything is real. When we wake up after dreaming, we have forgotten almost 90% of the dream. Have you ever thought that while we sleep, our eyes are closed. But we dream as if everything is in front of us, or rather, we are living a good life even in dreams, or rather, we are living better than that. But when the eyes open, it is just... it seems that why did we wake up. Well if I keep telling you about dreams, then this night and day will also end but these things will not end. If I explain to you in the language of science, you will not understand anything. Do you understand what I just told?" Pro. 'Shyamlal' asked.

"Something made sense." Abhay said.

“Anyway the subject of this dream is different, I just had to understand you because, when you see the memories on this machine, you will look like a dream. Although you will remember, you will not forget as much as you forget after waking up after dreaming. You will forget only less than that. Ok! Do not think much, just understand that, by saving your memory in this machine, you can see it anytime. If you forget your memory, you can see the saved one again. You can watch it no matter how many times. There is no limit in this. If you forget your memory, you can relive your memories by watching it again. And yes, whether that memory has gone into a car accident, or has gone due to a head injury, with this we can bring back our memory. This machine collects memories by scanning your memories and as we see the memories, we start remembering more memories. Similarly, all these memories are saved in this machine. And anyone can see these memories at any time."

“This is very good. That is, we can never forget our memory. ’Abhay‘ said happily with a little laugh.
"Yes !" ... ’Professor' said in agreement.

CHAPTER TWO

Golden Ball

"**But** I don't understand, why do you want to check my memory?" Abhay said hesitantly.

"We need you Mr. Sharma. You are the only one who can help us." Pro. 'Shyamlal' said.

"Help? How's the help?" 'Abhay' asked in surprise.

"To save the world."

"What! to save the world. But what is going to happen?" 'Abhay' asked.

"Through this book I came to know that the world is about to be destroyed. I found this book in the library when I was doing research on a book. There are some things in this that you should know. Yes! But this is not the whole point, some pages are torn. Pro. 'Shyamlal' said.

Pro. 'Shyamlal' gave that book to 'Abhay' to read. 'Abhay' started looking at that book very carefully. That book looked very old. The pages were too old. The words written in that book seemed ancient. Then 'Abhay' started reading the book.

(Written in that book...)

It is a matter of many thousand years ago, when deities, gods lived on the earth. Then they came to know that in the future the earth would be destroyed. That's why he had made such a golden ball, that he had put such a divine power in it, that the world could be saved, but this could be possible when all the planets came in a row when the sun's ray fell on it. If so, this could save the world.

Then 'Abhay' turns the page. There was a picture of him in that book, but the dress he wore was quite different. It looked very old. Abhay was very surprised to see that. And started looking at that picture carefully.

"This is your picture, from a previous life." Pro. 'Shyamlal' said 'Abhay' while looking at the picture carefully.

"What! my photo? my Rebirth? What are you saying this?" 'Abhay' was surprised and said with a disbelief.

"Yes, this is your reincarnation." When I got this book, I read this book but this book did not have complete information. It is further written in this book, that at that time the gods and goddesses had made three golden balls, and out of those three golden balls, one golden ball came to you, and without those three golden balls, the sun ray would have no effect and the whole That the whole world will be destroyed. And you had hidden a golden ball somewhere in it." Pro. 'Shyamlal' said.

"But why did I hide?" 'Abhay' asked in surprise.

"That's what we have to find out. Seeing your memory, why and how did you finally get this golden ball and why did you hide it? Pro. 'Shyamlal' said.

"But how can you say with so much certainty that this is my memory? Just because my face is bean, it will say little about my rebirth. And I don't even believe in reincarnation." Abhay said a little hesitantly.

"I know! It's a little hard to believe. But many such incidents have happened that it is a bit difficult to believe. ---- Then the professor showed some newspaper pages to

'Abhay'. There were many such news in that page which were incidents of reincarnation. 'Abhay' was a little surprised to read the page of that newspaper.

"When I read this book in full, that means half, then I felt that nothing can happen now, but one day I saw you in a coffee shop. Then I felt that maybe my eyes were deceiving, but I saw you right, that the picture I saw in this book was the same as you looked. Then I followed you where do you go? Where do you live? where do you work I found out everything and then one day it means tonight at 11:00 PM you were having fun in the club then I mixed sedation in your drink and after you fainted I brought you here. And you woke up thinking of a dream, it was not a dream, but it was a memory of a past life. Yes! Those were your memories. Everything will be shown to you like history, swords, old houses, villages, horses etc." Pro. 'Shyamlal' said.

Then 'Abhay' started trying to remember that dream. He started remembering something. He had seen something similar to what the 'Professor' had said. Then he nodded his head towards the 'Professor'.

"Yes! That's what I saw. But why did you kidnap me? You could have told me like that, what was the need to do all this?"

"If I had told you, you would not believe it and you would not be able to feel the way you are feeling now and it would have been better to come here and explain. And this machine could be understood only by looking at it. I'm sorry for this. I had no other choice."

"Never mind! You are right, maybe I really don't understand. And seeing all this, it means to believe..." "I am not able to understand what to say."

"Now understand everything by looking at the memories.

Then go see the memories?"
"Yes! Why not!..."

CHAPTER THREE

ASSASSIN'S TRAINING

'Nandani' starts the machine. Some codes started appearing on the computer screen in some English words. who were going from bottom to top and top to bottom.

"Lie down on this machine." 'Nandani' said 'Abhay' only while working on the machine.

'Abhay' was getting a little nervous. He walked very slowly and came near the machine.

"Do not panic! nothing will happen. You will see this like a dream. What you just saw a while back." 'Nandani' seeing 'Abhay' getting nervous said to him. ---- "Lie down quickly, I need to synchronize your memory."

Then 'Abhay' lies down on the machine. Then 'Nandani' puts the wire of the machine on the forehead of 'Abhay'. (With the help of that wire the memory of the brain is scanned and from that memory can be seen.) Then 'Nandani' asks 'Abhay' to close his eyes. Then some code starts moving up and down on the computer screen. Then the word Memory Synchronize appears on the computer screen. And those few lines start coming one after the other. Then the memory is synchronized.

Then in memory...

BC 1400 'Tikrit' A small town which was in 'Iraq'. The Sultan of 'Tikrit' was 'Rahim Khan'. He was a little dark in appearance. His age was clearly visible from his face. He was very old. He did not have a mustache, but his beard was very long and had a triangular shape from below. He used to wear a gray colored robe, on that robe a wonderful creation shone with a color like gold. and wore a gray royal cap on his head. And used to wear royal socks on the feet. He certainly looked like a great sultan. He had protected the Sultanate for many years. He had such an army of killers that, because of those killers, it was easy to protect the Sultanate. Whoever did wrong, these killers were used to kill them. That's why they were called murderers. And they were taught only here. He had to do whatever the Sultan said. And these killers considered Sultan 'Rahim Khan' as a god. And all the killers used to call the Sultan as 'Master'. These killers were only five. Assassins were trained to increase their numbers. All those killers wore the same clothes. He wore a white hooded cape, which ran from head to toe. Shoes were worn in black leather. And there was a small knife in the forearm, which was inside their clothes. It was easy for him to kill someone secretly. And one of those killers who was taking training, whose name was 'Jafir Ali', he was very special and the most unique was that the Sultan of 'Tikrit' believed to be 'Rahim Khan'. Because one day when all the killers were training, only then one of the killers means 'Jafir' who was facing a challenge.

(Training Class)

There was a big hall. There was a huge passage in that hall. There was a big statue on the side of that road. And there were many difficulties along the way. For example, if someone went ahead on that road, suddenly big swords and big hammers used to come out of a big idol. Who used to come in the middle of that road. And whoever went through that route, he had to escape from it. But this was a training class so it was all fake. But they were made in such a way that they all looked real. This training used to test the energy and skill of the killers. In such a situation, 'Jafir' was going to do this challenge for the first time. He was watching this challenge intently. And at that time Sultan 'Rahim' was also there and was watching everyone's challenge. If someone would go halfway and fall out after hitting a big sword, then if someone else went till the end, he would have been defeated with a hammer at n time. Then came the turn of 'Jafir'. Then 'Jafir' took a deep breath and then started facing the challenge. He started crossing it so fast that any sword and hammer and there were difficulties in winning it, 'Jafir' crossed it very easily. When there Sultan 'Rahim' was seeing 'Jafir' doing this, he could not believe his eyes. Because till date no one could overcome that challenge. And 'Jafir' had accomplished that in the very first time itself. Everyone was watching in amazement and everyone was applauding him for his feat. Then Sultan 'Rahim' called 'Jafir' to him.

"How did you do this? Till today no one could overcome this challenge but how did you complete it in one stroke?"

“Master I have a unique power. If an accident is happening to me, then at the time of that accident, I see everything in slow motion, that is why I can avoid any accident." Although 'Jafir' did not tell anyone about this power, but he had more faith in the Sultan, and considered him like a god, so he felt free to talk to the master.

On hearing this, Sultan 'Rahim' was very happy. Because they had to do a lot of work and that's why all those killers were being trained. And they had now found a killer who could do all these things.

The memory sequence ends one by one. And then Abhay wakes up.

"What happened? What did you see?" Pro. 'Shyamlal' asked 'Abhay'.

"I am a murderer. And there is a king 'of Tikrit city, his name is 'Rahim Khan' and my name is 'Jafir Ali'. I was being trained for killers." Then 'Abhay' tells all the things one by one. Whatever he saw in that memory sequence one, he tells everything to the 'Professor'.

Then 'Abhay' asks 'Professor', "But 'Professor' I do not understand one thing, I was talking in Arabic language but that I understood everything. How's that?"

"Oh! Well this is a very good thing. It's a little hard to say how do you understand this? But it's good that you understand. What is that, language is not meant to be understood but to be felt. Don't think how are you understanding it? Think you understand it. Just feel it, don't think too much." Prof. 'Shyamlal' said.

"You are right! Feeling it feels quite different. 'Professor' you can't understand how I feel right now."

CHAPTER FOUR

FOUR MURDERS

"**Are** you alright?" Pro. 'Shyamlal' put his hand on 'Abhay' shoulder and said.

"Yes! I'm all right." 'Abhay' said giving a smile.

"You take rest now, that's enough for today. 'Nandani' show this his room." Pro. 'Shyamlal' said.

'Nandani' shows 'Abhay' his room. Abhay goes to that room and sees the room. The room had a single bed for sleeping and a bathroom two steps to the right of it. And a small clock hung on the wall of the bedroom. However, there was not much in that room. There was no window in that room. That AC There was room. Which was just on and was running at about 18 degrees Celsius. That room was very cold. 'Abhay' took a look at that room.

"The room is nice! But it is quite small. 'Abhay' seeing the room said to 'Nandani'.

"Now go to sleep! It's 3 o'clock. it's so late. See you tomorrow morning." 'Nandani' while leaving said looking at the clock hanging on the wall. and closed the door.

'Abhay' felt a bit strange on this talk of 'Nandani'. She felt a little bad for not responding properly to him.

As soon as the door was closed, 'Abhay' saw that the door was locked with a digital code. Meaning if the door is to be opened, then the door will have to be opened with a digital code. Abhay was a little surprised to see this. That such a big building and such a small room and that too with digital lock, he got a little hesitant. But he was so tired now that he was sleeping a lot. He thought that I would talk to the 'Professor' about this tomorrow. Without thinking much, Abhay jumped on the bed and fell asleep.

Next morning 'Professor' came to his room, but 'Abhay' was still sleeping. It was 9 o'clock in the morning. Then the professor woke 'Abhay'.

"If you keep sleeping for so long, when will we see the memories?"

Abhay had woken up now. He yawned while getting up.

"Sorry! 'Abhay' said with embarrassment.

"Let's get ready now. We have a lot of memories to see." The professor said while leaving the room.

'Abhay' came to the hall getting ready, then 'Nandani' was doing some work looking at the machine's computer screen. 'Professor' was not in the hall. Seeing this, 'Abhay' came to Nandani. Was about to ask him something, that's when the 'Professor' came there.

"So you have come!" 'Professor' said. - "Let's turn on Nandini, it's too late." 'Professor' said while approaching the machine.

"I had to ask something." Abhay said.

"Ask! What is the matter?" 'Professor' said.

"Why is there a digital lock in my room?"

"The room here is like this. I just made this for safety. New age new technology. That's it, nothing else." 'Professor' said.

"May I know the lock code of my room?" Saying this, 'Abhay' looked at 'Professor' and 'Nandani' with suspicion. He felt that 'Professor' and 'Nandani' might not tell him.

Then 'Professor' saw 'Nandani'.

"What is lock code?" 'Professor' asked 'Nandani'.

"983624" said Nandani.

"Anything else to ask?" 'Professor' said.

Hearing this, Abhay was a bit shocked. It was the opposite of what he had thought, so he could not understand what to say now. He felt that the persecutor was doubting him. There is nothing that can be doubted.

"No!..." Abhay said embarrassedly. ---- And went and lay down on the machine.

Then 'Nandani' started the machine. The code started rolling up and down again on the computer screen.

Then in memory...

'Jafir' was called by 'Rahim' to his room. 'Rahim' was waiting for 'Jafir' to come from here to there and here and there. Rahim's room was very big. It was so big that the whole people used to hold their meeting there. If any decision had to be taken, it used to be here in this room. But today there was no one in the people. The only Sultan was 'Rahim'. Then 'Jafir' came to this room.

"come come! 'Jaffir' I was waiting for you only. I have one job for you. And only you can accomplish that." Seeing 'Jafir' coming, the Sultan 'Rahim' said.

"Say, what's the job Master?" 'Jafir' said, sitting on his knees, bowing his head.

'Jaffir' looked like 'Abhay' in appearance. Because of his clean shave, he looked even younger. His body was very rough. His age will be 26 or 27.

"get up! and come with me. You have something to show and something to tell."

Then Sultan 'Rahim' took 'Jafir' to another room. Where they were taken there only for certain works. And that room was a very secret place. And that room was very small. Then Sultan 'Rahim' told all the things about the destruction of the earth and the golden ball to 'Jafir'.

"You have to do one more thing for me. Think of it as part of a training.

"Where else is the Master?" 'Jafir' said.

"You have to kill four people. who do evil deeds. Black money, rigging of killers, kidnapping, plundering and the chieftain of all this 'Wasim Sheikh' who is the Sultan of 'Bhagdad' city. Right now you only have to kill those four people. And you will find them in the city of 'Bhagdad'. There you will find 'Husain Khan' who is a blacksmith. And he has a blacksmith shop. You have to go there. He will show you his picture and give his address." Rahim said.

"When do I have to go, Master?" 'Jafir' asked.

"You have to go today and now, because after this there is one more thing to do, that's why you have to go now." Rahim said.

"Okay Master!" 'Jafir' said.

'Jafir' did not ask many questions. That was it. And he used to consider Sultan 'Rahim' as a god, just as all the murderers believed in the same way. Because, that's what they were taught.

'Jafir' immediately pulled out from there. He took out his white horse and left for the city of 'Bhagdad'.

After coming near the city of Bhagdad, 'Jafir' saw the city. There were big walls around the city. There was a huge gate in front of the city and there were four guards. 'Jafir' could not go from the front. Then 'Jafir' started watching the city carefully. Then he thought that if he climbed the wall from another part of the city, then no one would be able to see him. Then 'Jafir' did the same, he slowly came to the other side of the city. The horse stayed there under a nearby tree. Then the wall started climbing. He was adept at such skill. He started climbing the wall very fast. Then 'Jafir' came inside the city. The city was very crowded. The people there were so busy in their work that they did not even know when 'Jafir' came inside the city after climbing the wall. 'Jafir' slowly started moving towards the city. Then to one of the men 'Jafir' asked the address of the shop of 'Husain Khan'.

***

There were many weapons made of iron in that shop. And some 2/3 men were making iron weapons. And some people were making the iron made of iron its sharp edge, while someone else was making the hammer. The sound of his making was echoing in the whole shop. Then someone called 'Husain Khan' seeing 'Jafir' asking.

"Say what do you want? Sword, Hammer, whatever wants here will be found here. All have sharp edges." 'Husain' said, showing the sword and hammer.

'Husain' was wearing a black robe. And there was a red cap on his head, which was shining brightly. Mojadis were worn on the feet. He was the owner of that shop, so he used to wear such clothes, so that he could be seen like the owner, that's why he used to wear such clothes.

"I have been sent by Sultan Rahim Khan." 'Jafir' said.

"Oh! Brother... we know. Rahim had told us that you are going to come today. How did we forget?... Excuse us. We come now." --- Then 'Husain' went inside. And came back after a while. But now he had some picture in his hand. Then he started showing the picture to 'Jafir'.

"This is 'Aasif Sheikh', it is he who manipulates the killers. and commits many crimes." 'Husain' was about to say something else that 'Jafir' interrupted him in the middle.

"That's all I know. Master has told me everything. Just tell me his address." 'Jafir' said.

"Which you there is a black market in the far back part of the city while there comes a right side way. There is his handcart, there he fiddles with the killers. 'Husain' said.

"Ok!" After saying this, 'Jafir' was leaving from there, when 'Husain' stopped him.

"Wait!... He'll need a good weapon to kill him. Wait, I'll give." 'Husain' was about to bring a good weapon saying that only then 'Jafir' stopped.

"No! There's no need for that." Then he took out a knife from the forearm of his hand and showed it to 'Husain'. "That's enough for him."

"Oh!... that's great." 'Husain' said smiling and happy. "But we should have asked for his head!"

"Ok. will get." Said 'Jafir' and left from there.

***

'Jafir' reached the place where 'Husain' had given the address of 'Asif Sheikh'. Asif was there. He was stuffing weapons in a box. And there were his companions who were filling other boxes with other weapons. There were a lot of boxes, which were full of weapons. 'Jafir' was watching all this from a far. Then 'Jafir' came to his base.

"You seem too early!" 'Jafir' seeing one of his companions filling the box said to them.

And then started killing his partner. Taking out the knife from his forearm, one by one from behind started directly putting the knife in the neck. By doing this, almost 3 or 4 of his companions were killed. In such a situation, 'Asif' saw and he started running from there. Then 'Jafir' also started running after him. 'Asif' was felt by part of the city's crowd. And 'Jafir' climbed through the walls of the houses of the city and started chasing 'Asif'. 'Jafir' was following him by leaping from one house to another. Then 'Asif' ran running and entered a corridor where no one was there. And got tired of running. And he stopped at one place and looked back and looked at 'Jafir'. Now he had dodged 'Jafir', so 'Asif' felt. But 'Jafir' was right on top of him. He was on the roof of a house and was watching her. Then 'Jafir' whistled and jumped on him. And put a knife in his neck.

***

'Jafir' did as 'Hussain' had said and put his head in front of 'Husain'.

"Oh! Brother, we thought that you would be too late, but you killed it very easily. And then the head was also laid. And that too soon. Seeing the head of 'Asif', 'Husain' said a little surprised. “We liked it very much. You have to kill 3 more people who do such bad things." 'Husain' said while taking out the picture of the other man. And then the picture of another man was shown to 'Jafir'.

Then 'Jafir' killed everyone like this one by one and brought their head to 'Husain'.

CHAPTER FIVE

BLACK MOUNTAIN

Suddenly 'Abhay' wakes up. And see that the machine was making noise and the color changed from blue to red. The machine suddenly broke down, that's why 'Abhay' suddenly woke up while looking at the memories.

"Every time something happens to it. How many times have I told you to close it properly while closing it." 'Professor' said angrily on 'Nandani'. "Now this machine will be operational only tomorrow. Ok! Let it be." Then looking at 'Abhay' he said, "Tell me what did you see?"

"What happened to this machine?" 'Abhay' seeing the machine shutting down and 'Professor' scolding 'Nandani' asked 'Professor'.

"Nothing! That machine got a little hot, that's why it is doing this. this will be fine. Tell me what did you see now?" 'Professor' asked 'Abhay'.

Then 'Abhay' told everything that he had seen in the memories.

"Ok! Can't do anything now. The memories ahead will probably have to be seen tomorrow only. Ok! So you rest. We'll talk tomorrow." Saying this the 'Professor' leaves from there.

Then 'Abhay' comes to 'Nandani' and asks her, "How long have you been working here?"

But 'Nandani' does not answer. She is closing the machine wire by putting it properly. Seeing 'Nandani' being ignored, 'Abhay' tells 'Nandani', "Look if you don't want to talk to me, it's okay! There is no coercion. Just..." 'Abhay' wanted to say something more, but he could not understand what to say and what to explain to her, so he was angry and was leaving from there.

"I work here for 2 years. Actually I was a student of professor. When I was in college, the professor used to teach science. I have learned a lot from him." Nandini said. Then he regretted that he had not spoken to Abhay properly. "Sorry... I shouldn't have behaved like that. What is it that, I am a little confused, that's why..." Nandani said embarrassedly.

"What is the matter? If there's a problem, you can tell me." Abhay said.

"Leave it! you tell! where did you study And what did you do?" 'Nandani' said with a view to changing the subject.

"You don't change things! What is the matter?" 'Abhay' interrupted to 'Nandani' and said.

"Nothing! Just... there is a little family problem and nothing else. Leave that, tell me where did you study?

Then 'Abhay' without thinking too much, he replied 'Nandani'.

"I don't even remember exactly that..."

"You haven't slept yet?" 'Professor' suddenly came there and said.

"No, that's me..." 'Abhay' said a little hesitantly.

"Ok! Now go to sleep. 'Nandani' I want to talk to you in private. Just come here." The professor said while cutting

'Abhay' in the middle.

'Abhay' started going to his room from there. While leaving, he was thinking that, what could be the problem of 'Nandani'? If he has a family problem, then who will be in his family? And what would be the problem? Many such questions were coming in his mind. He wanted to go and ask her now, but he could not do so because 'Professor' had suddenly come there. And he did not think it right to tell 'Professor'. That's why he went quietly to his room. While going to his room, he saw 'Nandani' and 'Professor' going to another room which was right next to his room. Then 'Abhay' started hearing some sound which was coming from other room. And that voice was of 'Professor' and 'Nandani'. who was speaking in the other room. 'Abhay' was hearing that voice because there was a hot air heater in that room which was on the same wall where that other room was. And his connection used to go to the same other room, so some sound was being heard from that room. However, he could not hear clearly. It was just getting to know from him that 'Professor' was getting a little angry and scolding 'Nandani'. Then for a moment 'Abhay' felt that, just now by going to that room, I should ask 'Professor' why he is scolding 'Nandani'? Then he thought that it would not be right to do so. They will not answer me properly. Then 'Abhay' thought that if 'Nandani' got him alone tomorrow, then I would ask what could be the reason for 'Professor" scolding him. "Yes! That would be right." He said in his mind. And then went to sleep on the bed. But he could not sleep. Then he looked at the clock hanging on the wall and it was 2 o'clock in the afternoon. Then lying on the bed, he started thinking that what is Manjra? Why was 'Professor' scolding 'Nandani'? And what could be Nandani's problem?

Then after some half an hour, he fell asleep while thinking of 'Abhay' lying down. He didn't even know when he got his eyes.

Then after 2/4 hours 'Nandani' came to pick up 'Abhay' in his room. Abhay was sleeping very soundly.

"Let's get up early, the machine is on." 'Nandani' said to 'Abhay'.

'Abhay' suddenly woke up from sleep after hearing the voice of 'Nandani'. Then he yawned. While yawning, he saw 'Nandani' going out of his room. And he too came after him in a hurry. He was a little worried about the morning. And he wanted to ask 'Nandani' something. When he came out of his room into the hall, he saw that the 'Professor' was also standing in the hall waiting for him.

"Let's sit down soon! We look forward to memories." The 'Professor' seeing 'Abhay' coming in the hall said to him.

Seeing 'Professor', 'Abhay'' face dropped a bit. He fell silent. And came and stood near the machine. Now he could not speak anything to 'Nandani' even if he wanted to. I don't know why he was not getting the courage to say anything to 'Nandani' in front of 'Professor'. He was not feeling well now. He thought that after seeing this last memory, he would now go straight to Nandani and talk to Nandni about what is the problem with you. And why was the 'Professor' scolding you?

"Let's sit down now." 'Nandani' spoke to 'Abhay' only while working on the computer screen of the machine.

Hearing the voice of 'Abhay' 'Nandani', his attention came out of his mind. And then he went and lay down on the machine.

The codes started running from top to bottom on the computer screen.

Then in memory...

Jafir killed all four of them and entered the Sultan's chamber. Sultan 'Rahim' was very happy. It was clearly visible from the smile on his face. Sultan 'Rahim' had not done any mistake, entrusted this work to 'Jafir'.

"come come..! 'Jafir' I am very happy. You did this job very well." 'Rahim' seeing 'Jafir' coming into the room said to him.

"Thank you Master." 'Jafir' said, sitting on his knees, greeting.

"Now get up and come with me. There is still other work to be done." Saying this 'Rahim' took 'Jafir' to the secret room.

After coming to the secret room, Sultan Rahim draws out a map. And keep it on a big table.

"What I told you about the golden ball, here is the map. This is the black mountain. Rahim said, placing his hand on the map, showing the black mountain. "You have to go here. There is a golden ball in this black mountain. which you have to bring. There you may have to face a lot of difficulties. Just like you did in training. That's how you have to deal with it. No one could go there till today. Now everything is up to you. I have two golden balls, this is the last one left. which you have to bring. And only you can do this through that power."

"Yes! Master, I will do this, you don't worry about this. But I do not understand why the golden ball is kept in such a place?"

"All this because of the sultan of that Bhagdad city, he thinks it belongs to God. We cannot insult God by taking him."

"Meaning!"

"Meaning! Who will explain to him that God has given it only to save it. In that golden ball, divine power has been cast to save the world."

"May I talk to him?"

"Even you let it be 'Jafir' nothing is going to happen to him. We have to do this work like this. So are you ready?"

"Ok! Master I am ready. It will be as you say." Saying this 'Jafir' immediately came out to get the golden ball.

***

'Jafir' comes to that black mountain through the map. 'Jafir' starts watching that black mountain from afar. The black mountain was very high. Its big pancakes were full of black colour. It was Shyam's time. The sun had come very close to the earth from the sky. Now it seemed that the sun would now set after some half an hour. A slight ray of sun was falling on that black mountain.

Then 'Jafir' kicked the horse and made it run fast and started towards the black mountain. Then as soon as he came inside the black mountain, that horse kept him at a place somewhere. And 'Jafir' started going inside alone.

After going some distance, he saw a big path. On the right side of that road and on the left side there were huge statues, which were going in one line all the way. And she was looking very attractive. The length of that idol was about 50 feet. Just as the idol was there at the time of 'Jafir' training, it was here. After coming there, 'Jafir' started watching that road carefully. And getting ready to go that route. Then 'Jafir' slowly started moving forward. As he came in the middle of that idol, he started seeing big swords coming down. And this was looking at him very slowly. Then 'Jafir' started running. He started going ahead even before the big swords came down from the idols. With this 'Jafir' started shining all the swords and hammers and started moving forward. He didn't even get a scratch. And he started crossing quite easily.

After dodging the huge statues and swords, he stood just a short distance away from the golden ball. But there were two guards. Seeing him, they started attacking him. Then 'Jafir' started killing those people. After hitting him, he stood near the golden ball and started looking at it.

CHAPTER SIX

The Truth Of The Golden Ball

The golden ball was like a pillar and was on a long stone. On top of it was a large round stone, a golden ball was placed on it. The golden ball was shining brightly. The light of the golden ball was falling on that round shaped stone.

Then 'Jafir' picked up that golden ball. As soon as he picked up the golden ball, the long pillar-like stone started going down. And then a strange rumbling sound started coming in the black mountain. Like an earthquake is happening.

"Who are you? And how did you even get there?" One of the two guards said the wounded soldier.

'Jafir' just kept staring at him. And then he started leaving.

"Stop! Who are you and why are you taking it?" said the wounded soldier.

"I have very little time. I have to save the world." Saying this 'Jafir' started leaving from there.

Then some more 2/4 soldiers came there. And surrounded 'Jafir' from all sides. 'Jafir' started looking at them all.

"Let me go! I want to save the world. Leave my way." Saying this, while holding the golden ball in one hand, he took out a knife from the arm of the other hand.

"What? What does it mean to save the world? What is the relation of the golden ball and the world with this? The wounded soldier got up and said.

"Is none of your business!" 'Jafir' said angrily.

"How not to do it! I've protected it for many years."

"Meaning?" 'Jafir' said in surprise.

"I mean I'll tell you." Suddenly a man came standing behind the golden ball and said.

'Jafir' was a little surprised to see them. He suddenly came that way. Where the golden ball was kept. And some soldiers had also come earlier through the same route and had surrounded 'Jafir'. 'Jafir' could not understand anything. In this situation, he could not even run away from there.

The man was wearing a blue robe. And a blue royal cap was worn on his head. He looked just like a sultan in appearance.

"You?" 'Jafir' asked the questioner.

"I'm 'Mohammed Khan'." Saying this 'Mohammed' stops for a while and he has some doubts and he asks 'Jafir' to know there, "So you 'Rahim Khan' has sent, to get this golden ball?"

"Yes... I want to save the world, but you won't let me. That's why the master has sent me to get this golden ball."

"What! Who told you that the world is going to be destroyed? Nothing is going to happen to the world. 'Rahim' has lied to you."

"Master never lie. I have full faith in them."

"Ok! So what has your master told you?"

"Why should I tell you, I don't have time, let me go."

"Now I understand, then you are the one who killed our four soldiers?"

"Yes! But here, black money, rigging of killers, kidnapping and many such illegal things are done here. And his chieftain who is the sultan of this city 'Wasim Sheikh'."

"Ok! Then who am I?"

"What do you mean?"

"Means this is the Sultan of this city 'Mohammed Khan'. Said a soldier standing there.

"Yes! I am Sultan 'Mohammed Khan' and 'Rahim Khan' is my elder brother."

"What!" 'Jafir' was quite surprised to hear this.

"Yes! This is a matter of that time, when elder brother lived with us and our father used to protect the sultanate. Our father's name was Sultan 'Abdul Khan'. He was very unique. He had a lot of respect. Everyone considered our father like a god. Because, he took care of the people very well. and protected the Sultanate. He had 2 wives. The first Begum's son was Rahim Khan and I was the second Begum's son. 'Rahim' was the first child of this family, that is why he was raised with a lot of pampering. And because of this pampering, 'Rahim' was quite stubborn and angry. He was very dear to his mother. But when Rahim's mother suddenly fell ill. Then the mother of 'Rahim' asked the father for one last wish and that was to see 'Rahim' as the Sultan of this city. His father did not approve of this, because 'Rahim' was not worthy of him that much. Father believed so. He was very stubborn and angry. And this was not what my father liked. But he had to obey his words in front of his Begum. Then one day 'Rahim' was declared as

Sultan.

“Then after a few days, the father came to know that all this was a plan made by Rahim, to demand the Sultan of this city by making his mother pretend to be ill. Because before this Rahim had proposed to his father many times to be his Sultan. But my father flatly refused. Rather he had said, "I will make my second son the Sultan, but not you." The same thing bothered ’Rahim‘ a lot, that he was more attached to me than ’Rahim‘. ’Rahim‘ used to be very jealous of me because my father loved me more than ’Rahim‘. There was a reason for this too, because when I was born. So after a few days my mother passed away. And after that I was raised by my father. I was very dear to my father. He loved me very much. It was his heart’s wish that after him I would become the Sultan of this city. Because, I had all the qualities needed for the Sultan of a city. Dad thought so."

“When he came to know that it was all drama. So father got very angry and scolded ’Rahim‘’s mother a lot and then ’Rahim‘ too. Dad was very angry with both of them. Then I asked my father to forgive him. But the father was not ready to accept it. But then I begged a lot, then my father agreed. And ’Rahim‘ became the Sultan of this city and started protecting the Sultanate."

“Then many days passed. Then one day the father came to know about the black deeds of ’Rahim‘, he was stunned to hear this. He used to manipulate the killers with the enemies and do black business. He was taking advantage of being the Sultan of this city. He used to do all this after beating him. Then ’Rahim‘ was called to the father’s room, although there was no one else there except his close friends. Father was so angry that he wanted to punish Rahim in the prison. If this thing spreads outside, then all the respect that my father had earned will be found in ruins. That's why dad's friend said that all these things should not be spread outside. But my father flatly refused. He knew that if he forgave it again this time, it would do worse. That is why father asked 'Rahim' to leave the city. And asked to say in the city that now the sultan of this city is no more in this world, he was killed in a warrior. And now the next Sultan is 'Mohammed Khan'."

"Then the very next day Dad fell very ill. Then when he was taking his last breath, he told me about the golden ball. He had found that golden ball in a mountainous area. There was a button in the middle of that golden ball. If it is pressed, a goddess will appear and tell about the power of that golden ball. If the ray of that sun falls on this golden ball at the time of solar eclipse, then you will get one of your will power and the boon of being immortal. All this was told to me by my father before his passing when he was ill. He did not have enough time now that he could stay till the solar eclipse. That is why he told me all these things and gave me the responsibility of handling this sultanate. Because he had more faith in me. He did not even tell this thing to 'Rahim'. But when he was telling me this, Rahim was somewhere in the same corner. And he listened to everything. and left this city. But Rahim had to get the golden ball. And for this he made a lot of efforts. But there was still a long time for the solar eclipse. So that's why it was very important to keep this golden ball somewhere. Then I brought it to such a place that no one can get it. Then when I saw this black mountain, I had to create difficulties for him here. Rahim tried a lot to bring this golden ball, but also made an army of many killers to reach here and also trained them, but till date no one has reached here except you, how did you do it?"

'Jafir' told about his power to 'Mohammed'.
"Oh! Now I understand why Rahim chose you? Because, only you could cross this path. That's why 'Rahim' got you to do this work and got our man killed too." 'Mohammed' said.
"Then who were those four men?" 'Jafir' asked.

"He was our own man. He didn't do any illegal work. Rather, we had prepared that man to kill 'Rahim'. But 'Rahim' has used you cleverly and destroyed the plans of our own man. But who told you the addresses of our four men?"

"He is a blacksmith living in your own city. He has a blacksmith shop. His name is 'Husain Khan'.

"I knew a man from Raheem was watching over us. But I didn't know who he was. Rahim has told you everything a lie. He is a master of story making. He knows it very well to lie."

"That means nothing is going to happen to the world?" 'Jafir' asked in surprise after hearing this talk of 'Mohammed'.

"Yeah... nothing's going to happen, it's all a lie."

"That is, those 3 golden balls and that..."

"It's all a lie. There is no other golden ball, it is just one golden ball." 'Mohammed' cut the words of 'Jafir' in the middle and said.

"Is there really only one golden ball? No more golden balls?" 'Jafir' still could not believe it. That's why he asked so.

"Yeah... there is no other ball. Has 'Rahim' shown you any golden ball?" 'Jafir' seeing 'Mohammed' asking like this asked him. Because he knew that there is no golden ball. And he also knew what the answer of 'Jafir' was going to come now. He just asked this for his satisfaction.

"No! He didn't show any golden ball."

The same answer of 'Jafir' came as they thought.

Then all of a sudden the mountain's spines started shaking. And some stones started falling from above and only then 'Jafir' fell on one side and 'Mohammed' and soldiers fell on the other side. 'Jaafir' and 'Mohammed' lost contact now. Because, big stones had fallen from above and had made a big wall. His voice was not even reaching 'Jaafir' and the voice of 'Jafir' was not reaching him. But the golden ball was still with 'Jafir'.

CHAPTER SEVEN

FINAL

'Abhay' woke up seeing the memories. And got up and sat down on the machine itself.

"What happened? What did you see?" The 'Professor' asked 'Abhay' as soon as he got up from the machine.

But 'Abhay' did not react. Rather, he could not hear anything. Seeing the memories, he was immersed in his own thoughts.

"What happened? Tell me... what did you see?" 'Professor' asked again.

He said hurriedly, "I went to the black mountain where the golden ball was kept. And..." 'Abhay' stopped in the middle as soon as he said this. He did not even notice that before telling all this, 'Professor' should ask and then 'Abhay' started looking towards 'Professor'. He just stared at the 'Professor' for a while. Because, seeing the memories he had seen, he was doubting the 'Professor'. Many questions were echoing in his mind. Then he asked 'Professor', "What are you hiding from me 'Professor'? You told the truth... what are you hiding from me?"

"What do you mean? Why would I hide something? Tell me what did you see? You found the golden ball that was in the black mountain. Could you go there?" The 'Professor' asked curiously.

"Leave all that, first you tell me what you are hiding from me. That golden ball doesn't do what you told me. Neither the world is going to be destroyed, you are hiding something or the other. You don't want to take that golden ball to save the world but for your own benefit. I just don't understand how do you know all this? You must know something or the other that you are hiding from me.

"said! Now go away, if you don't tell then I only see your memories. Start 'Nandani'!" Saying this 'Professor' was coming to the machine, that's when 'Abhay' starts killing the machine. and cuts its wire. And also breaks the computer screen and ruins the whole machine.

Seeing this the 'Professor' gets very angry. "What have you done? Why did you do this?"

"Now only I know where is that golden ball? If you want to know? So first of all you tell me the truth and What are you hiding from me?"

The Professor was looking at Abhay angrily.

"Ok! If I don't tell then what will you do?"

Then 'Abhay' picks up a pencil lying on the computer table. And holding hands towards them like a knife. "If you don't tell, you'll never know where that golden ball is. Only I know where that golden ball is. And you can't do anything except me."

The face of the 'Professor' was now very red with anger. Now he could not do anything even if he wanted to. Because the machine was now broken. And only now 'Abhay' knew about the golden ball.

Then the professor started telling, "I am 'Rahim Khan'. I have been reborn."

'Abhay' was shocked to hear this. He just stared at the professor.

"When I was little, I used to see these memories in my dreams. But it became difficult to remember more blurry. Then after I grew up I did a lot of research. Is reincarnation a truth or a lie? When I found many cases which were of reincarnation. And went to the place where I was born last. And the place where the golden ball was. But now it was all in ruins. And because the memories were blurry, I could not remember much where was the golden ball? And then after I studied, when I became a scientist, I started working on the memory recall machine. This machine was very important, why it was necessary to see the memories and that too from the past life then it took me 30 years to make this machine. I spent half my life in this machine. And then one day it came when this machine was completely made, then I saw the memories of my previous life in this machine, but I had the memories of my past life in my mind but the golden ball was with you. Despite making the machine, I could not find the golden ball. The memory of the golden ball was in your mind. And my 30 years of hard work had now gone in vain. And I had given up hope. In this birth, it had become very difficult to get the golden ball. But one day I saw you in a coffee shop. You were seen in the same way as the one I saw you in the memories of the previous life. And then a glimmer of hope arose. And I was hoping that you too would be reborn. May the memories of this past life be there in your mind as well. Then I followed you where do you live? where do you work Knew everything. Then got a fake book made, you know that nowadays everything is available and anything can be made. Similarly, I made a book that looks like an old one and printed some half and got some pages torn. The book was made in such a way that it looked like a very old one and which 'Rahim' meant that what I had told in my previous life that the world is going to be destroyed, in the same way I got it printed on this book as if it seemed to be true. And put your picture too. Because you take it for granted. I had to do all this to persuade you. And I kept such evidences that all this seems true to you. What needed to be done. Because it was necessary to make you believe something. I knew it was not a day's work to see these memories. Who only after making you unconscious after bringing you here and seeing the memories, could take you back to the same place from where you had fainted. Although I wanted to do it there. But you woke up And this book was very important for you to understand. And yes there was another reason for fainting, I had sedated you because it was very important to see whether the memories of your past lives are in your mind or not. If you didn't have memories in your mind, I wanted to bring you home comfortably. without telling you But I was lucky that you had memories of past lives in your mind. And as soon as you got up, I had to tell you slowly and you already know."

"And 'Nandani'? Is this really a research assistant or someone else? 'Abhay' looked at 'Nandani' and asked.

'Nandini' lowered her face in embarrassment. And stood silently.

"What am I asking? Answer me." 'Abhay' shouted.

"I'm not a research assistant." Nandani broke her silence. "I was just a student of 'Professor', I was in dire need of money. I had to save my brother. He has brain tumour. I didn't have that much money for his treatment. And then one day 'Professor' came to meet me and told everything. And he said that he will bear all the expenses to save my brother. And he did not want to harm anyone and did not want to make me do bad work, so thinking of this, I agreed to work with 'Professor'.

"And I needed to take care of you. Because I knew that, when you start seeing memories, then one day or the other memories will appear in dreams. Because the same thing happened to me, but it didn't happen to you. Neither did you tell me anything nor to 'Nandani'..." said the 'Professor'. "I had a dream. 'Abhay' said while cutting the professor in the middle. I just didn't tell this thing and I started doubting from the very day when you were scolding 'Nandani' in a room. I just wanted to get to the bottom of this. And wanted to know your truth. Why were you scolding her then?"

"That I was scolding because 'Nandani' was talking to you excessively. She was not caring about her work. And you were trying to get closer to her. I did not want that my whole plan should get spoiled after coming here. And she was insisting on meeting her brother. It was not right for me to leave you alone and send her to the hospital. So that's why I had to scold her." After saying this the 'Professor' remained silent for a while. Then after a while, "Now everything has been told to you, now tell me where is the golden ball?"

"I won't tell. I don't want you to get that. Wherever he is, he is safe. No one can take him away from there."

"You tell or not. The 'Professor' got very angry. And they started coming towards 'Abhay' to attack him with anger. Then 'Abhay' took his pencil on the arm of his hand and held it like a knife, and 'Professor' came in front of him and inserted the pencil in his stomach. And then put that pencil in his pocket. And the 'Professor' became covered in blood. And fell down in agony and died.

'Nandani' was very nervous seeing all this. She was so nervous that her hands and feet were trembling.

"Do not panic! I didn't want to kill them. They suddenly came to attack me. So I had to do it in my own defence."

'Abhay' said explaining his point to 'Nandani'.

"Now?" Nandini said.

"Nothing will happen. We have to get out of here quickly." Saying this 'Abhay' came to 'Nandani'. And got hold of her. She was very scared. Slowly he started taking her out of the room. Then asked 'Nandani' to pack his things. He could not leave Nandani in this condition and go alone from there. And he had now got all the answers about the 'Nandani' going on in his mind. He had pity for her, so he wanted to take Nandani away from here as well.

'Nandani' packed her things and came to the hall. Abhay was waiting for him standing in the hall itself. Suddenly 'Nandani' remembered about the golden ball and asked 'Abhay', "That golden ball? Where is he at?"

"This is safe now. No one can take this. Don't worry about this. Just get out of here now." Saying this 'Abhay' took 'Nandani' away from there.

***

'Nandani' and 'Abhay' were in the hospital. 'Nandani' brother's treatment was now done. The 'Professor' had also given his money. And now he was going to be discharged. His brother was only 13 years old. He looked exactly like 'Nandani' in appearance. His life was now saved because of 'Professor'.

At the same time, on the TV of the hospital, a woman was giving news on the news channel that, "The famous scientist 'Shyamlal Mehta' has been murdered. He was found covered in blood in his building. Who did the murder, it is not yet known. The investigation is still on."

'Nandani' and 'Abhay' were watching the news. And 'Nandani' was looking very scared seeing this news. On the spot 'Abhay' seeing 'Nandani' getting nervous tried to pacify her.

Then after coming out of the hospital.

"Ok! I’ll leave now. If we ever meet again, we will meet. The charge of blood will not come on you. Because there is no evidence against you. And if I get caught, they will never be able to catch me. If you are investigated, just tell me what you know. Don’t worry about my getting caught, tell me whatever is true. Abhay said.

"I can’t do that."

’Abhay‘ looked at ’Nandani‘, she stood looking down in despair. He had to say one thing that he thought he could say now. "I had to tell you one thing. You asked about that golden ball, not what I said it was safe now."

"Hmm!" Nandani said yes in agreement.

"Actually that’s what I used to do. I am ’Jafir Aali‘. I am immortal now." ’Abhay‘ (Jafir) said.

’Nandani‘ was quite surprised to hear this. She was looking at him in surprise.

"Yes! I am ’Jafir Aali‘." ’Abhay‘ (Jafir) said.

"Yes! I am ’Jafir Aali‘." ’Abhay‘ (Jafir) said.

In the memory of the previous birth, speak of ’Abhay‘.

When the crest of the mountain shook, ’Jafir‘ fell on the other side and ’Mohammed‘ and his soldiers fell on the other side. Then the voice of ’Jafir‘ was not reaching them and neither the voice of ’Mohammed‘ was reaching ’Jafir‘. Then ’Jafir‘ came out of that mountain and ran away from there. When he left that city and village and came out somewhere far away, he pressed the button of that golden ball. On pressing it, a goddess appeared and that goddess started telling about the power of that golden ball. Hearing this, ’Jafir‘ took that golden ball at the time of solar eclipse, as soon as the sun’s rays fell on that golden ball, he tried his strength and himself became immortal and had to ask for a will power which he asked to protect this world for years

and years. Keep it nothing happen.
Hearing this, Nandani's senses were blown away. She was just staring at 'Abhay'. And then suddenly she said, "That means you have not been reborn. It's you, it's your memories.

"Yes!" 'Abhay' (Jafir) nodded.

"Then why didn't you tell this to 'Professor'?" 'Nandani' asked 'Abhay' (Jafir).
"They do not listen to me, on the contrary, they get very angry. For whom he did so much, if he had come to know that he would never get it, then he would have killed me.
"What are you talking about, now you have become immortal, haven't you? So how could he kill you?"

"No it is not so. I can die if my accident or someone hits me then I can die. I can never get old. I have become immortal only in the body. And the power I had before is gone now. To appear slow at the time of the accident. I have gained one power and have lost one."

"Then why don't you remember? And how are you living with this name?"
"I don't know that either. Maybe because of this I do not remember that no one can live so many years, but I am living. It would have been difficult to remember so many years. That's why I don't remember all this. And I don't even remember how I started the life of this name. Only that machine could answer it. And now I ruined that too."
After being silent for a while, Abhay said again, "So you don't have to worry about me. If the police come to you while investigating, then tell me straight away. Yes! Just don't say that I am 'Jafir Aali'. After saying this 'Nandani' started laughing. "Just tell him here why you worked with 'Professor'. Don't worry about me, nothing will happen to me. What is it, that the police will not understand this.

"No, I won't tell them anything. But where will you go now?" Nandani asked worriedly.

"Leave this city and go to start a new life. Maybe I've been here for so long. That's why I am living by this name. But this time I will try to remember who I am. And when I get bored with life, one day I will be free from my life. Well then! See you." Saying this, 'Abhay' shook hands with 'Nandani' for the last time and started leaving from there. And 'Nandani' just kept watching him go. She also wanted to get away from this trouble now. Somewhere far away with his brother and he did the same there. She also went somewhere far away.

THE END

9 798886 065145

Printed by Libri Plureos GmbH in Hamburg,
Germany